The Rand McNally Book of Favorite Animal Stories

RAND McNALLY & COMPANY Chicago

Established 1856

**This book contains the stories THE LITTLE MAILMAN
OF BAYBERRY LANE, FOREST BABIES, LITTLE BOBO AND
HIS BLUE JACKET and MOMMY CAT AND HER KITTENS,**
copyright © by Rand McNally & Company in 1952,
1949, 1953 and 1959 respectively. 1980 Edition.
Printed in U.S.A.

Library of Congress Catalog Card Number: 80-50661

CONTENTS

The Little Mailman of Bayberry Lane

IT WAS a lovely, clear, autumn morning in Bayberry Lane. The trees were bright yellow and red. The thistles were sparkling with dew. And there was that good bayberry smell coming from the bushes on either side of the lane.

Even though it was very early, Mrs. Goose had wandered far up the lane picking bayberries. She was going to make bayberry candles that day. Besides, she always liked to be the first to welcome the Little Mailman, for he had the latest gossip. She peered up the lane to see if he was in sight.

Mrs. Duck was sweeping the yellow leaves off her walk. She, too, kept going out to her mailbox and looking up the lane. "I do hope there's a letter from my sister," she thought.

Mr. Turtle was sitting on his front step in the warm sunshine. His eyes were closed, but he wasn't asleep. He was listening for the cheery whistle of the Little Mailman. "I wonder if he'll bring my new tulip catalog," he thought.

But he didn't go out to the gate and look up the lane. "Shucks!" he said, "What's the hurry . . . . anyhow!"

Around the bend in the lane was Mrs. Pig's house. Mrs. Pig was waiting by her mailbox, even though she never received any letters. Every morning she hoped for one, but every morning the Little Mailman passed her by.

Then from up the lane came the Little Mailman's chatter. "Ah, Mrs. Goose, you're out early this morning! Here is your mail. Have you heard that the Robins are going south for the winter?

"And, Mrs. Duck, a yellow letter for you today. Yellow means good news, you know!"

He put a tulip catalog into Mr. Turtle's mail-box and called, "Hi, Mr. Turtle! Here are tu-lips for you that won't talk back! Ha! Ha! Ha!"

And, as quickly as he had come, he was around
the bend in the lane. There he slowed down to a
walk and his cheerfulness seemed to leave him.
He didn't like to go by Mrs. Pig's house. He
couldn't bear the look of disappointment on her
face every morning. The Little Mailman was the
only one who guessed how sad and lonely Mrs.
Pig was.

And there she was, standing by her mailbox,
waiting for him.

The Little Mailman put on a bright smile and called, "Good morning, Mrs. Pig! Say, do I smell *apple tarts* this morning?"

"I have one here for you," said Mrs. Pig. "Today's my baking day, you know."

He bit into the tart. "*M-m-m-m-m-m!* Mrs. Pig, you're the very best cook in Bayberry Lane!"

Mrs. Pig blushed and looked very pleased. And with a cheery, "Thank you," the Little Mailman bounded off down the lane.

He thought, "I wonder why Mrs. Pig never gets any letters. Maybe it's because she never writes any herself. I wonder why she doesn't have any *friends*. Maybe it's because she never goes out anywhere to *make* friends. Maybe she's shy and afraid to try. Somebody ought to get her started! I wish I could think of some way to help her."

He was still munching the apple tart. "Hm-m-m-m!" he said. "Today is Friday. I wonder what she'll bake *next* Friday!" Then he had a wonderful idea. "Wonderful!" he shouted. And he couldn't wait to get home to start working on it.

The Little Mailman's house was under a stone wall, so it was always dark in his rooms, even in the middle of the day. He lighted one of Mrs. Goose's bayberry candles and sat down at his table to write.

He wrote, "You are invited to a surprise party for Mrs. Pig, next Friday afternoon at three." Then he popped the invitation into a pink envelope for Mr. and Mrs. Goose. Then another for the Ducks, and one for Mr. Turtle.

The next morning, after the Little Mailman had passed through Bayberry Lane, all was excitement. Everyone but Mrs. Pig had received a pink invitation. There hadn't been a party in the lane for a long time.

Mrs. Goose was ironing her party sash.

Mrs. Duck was sticking new feathers in her party hat.

And Mr. Turtle was shaking mothballs out of the pockets of his party jacket.

But Mrs. Pig was still sad and lonesome as she went about her housework.

On Friday she did her baking as usual. This time she made apple tarts and little lemon cakes all covered with hickory nuts. She set them on the windowsill to cool and went out to work in the garden.

At three o'clock she was just picking a bouquet of chrysanthemums when she heard, "SURPRISE! SURPRISE!" And up popped six heads from her garden wall!

She dropped the flowers, and dropped the scissors, and stood with her mouth wide open. She could hardly believe her eyes.

Then she remembered her manners and said, "Oh, do come in, won't you?"

They all scrambled over the stone wall, all except Mr. Turtle who went around and through the gate.

Mrs. Goose said, "I've brought you one of my handmade bayberry candles. They smell so good when they're burning!"

Mrs. Duck said, "I've brought you a feather duster I made myself."

The Little Mailman had brought her a basket of hickory nuts.

And just then Mr. Turtle arrived and presented her with one of his best tulip bulbs.

It was the happiest afternoon of Mrs. Pig's life,

But a bear who is going everywhere has to go somewhere, so Buffin forgot the hurt and went on till he smelled honey in the air.

The nice smell was coming from a tall tree.

"Sniff, sniff, and up I go!" said Buffin to himself, and up he went. There, sure enough, was a hole in the tree, and honey smells coming out of it. Buffin put his nose in for a lick of honey, but the bees would not have such doings in their tree!

"*Ouch! Ouch!*" cried Buffin, climbing down backward as fast as he could. Just before he reached the bottom, he took a back somersault and landed WHOP! in the thickest cocklebur patch in the whole forest.

"A pretty how-de-do!" said Buffin, as he crawled out with the burs sticking to his fur. His nose was *really* hurting this time, and he held it with one paw while he ran on the other three straight to the little pond and rolled around in the cool mud—because all bears know that mud is good for stings.

"What strange animal is this coming up our path?" said Father Bear when he saw Buffin.

Mother Bear started picking out the burs and scraping off the mud and rubbing the stings with honey.

When the mud was out of his ears, they said, "Where *have* you been?"

"Everywhere," Buffin said in a little voice.

The next morning Buffin crawled out of bed, rubbed his nose, and said to his father, "Let's go honeying *together* today!"

And while his father was waking up and getting started, he heard Buffin say as cheerily as ever, "Hello, World!"

ROLY AND POLY GET DIZZY

THE raccoon twins looked so much alike that no one could tell which was which. Roly had a high forehead—but then, so did Poly! Poly had bright eyes—but then, so did Roly!

When the animals in the forest asked Roly how *he* could tell which was which, he just said, "Well, you see, Poly has a Poly look, and I haven't."

And when they asked Poly, he said, "It's very simple. Roly has a Roly look, and I haven't."

So Roly and Poly never got mixed up, but everyone else did.

On the slope of Rushing Brook there was an old hollow log where Roly and Poly went to play every day. Roly would hide very quietly, and when Poly found him they would roll around and pommel each other and giggle. Then it would be Poly's turn to hide.

Then they would chase each other into one end of the old log and out of the other end. Once their noise woke up Sleepy Owl in the oak tree. He peered out and watched them for a long time. Then he shook his head and said, "I never saw a raccoon run so fast in all my life. Right while he's going in one end, he's coming out the other!"

With that Roly and Poly stopped, and he saw that there were two of them.

"How do you know which is yourself, or don't you?" he said.

But Roly only looked at Poly and said, "He's the one with the Poly look."

As the twins grew older and stronger, they ran so fast through the hollow log that it fairly trembled and shook. One day they ran through it, round and round, a *hundred times*.

"A hundred and one," puffed Roly.

"A hundred and two," puffed Poly.

But on the "hundred and three" they both fell to the ground, as dizzy as May flies, and lay looking up at the sky.

"The clouds are whirling round and round," said Roly.

"The ground is going up and over," said Poly.

Then they heard their mother calling, and they got up and went plunging and tumbling along the bank of the brook toward home. When they passed the quiet pool, Roly stopped to look at himself. He was so dizzy he didn't know whether he was upside down or not!

"Is that you or I?" he said.

"It's you," said Poly who, by now, was not quite so dizzy.

"How can you tell?" said Roly.

"Because you have a Roly look," said Poly.

"That's all right then—as long as you're sure. It would be awful if *we* got mixed up about it!"

And they ran on home, tumbling over each other and giggling all the way.

LITTLE DEER GETS A NAME

WHEN Little Deer was only a few days old, he looked up at his mother and said, "Why can't I have a name all my own—like Buffin and Bunnifer? No one calls Buffin, 'Little Bear,' or Bunnifer, 'Little Rabbit'! Why must I always be called 'Little Deer'?"

"Well, you see, it's this way," answered his mother. "We deer have to earn our names. 'Flash' was named that because he can run so fast. 'Lightfoot' earned his name because his feet hardly touch the ground. And 'Long Antlers' grew the longest antlers."

Little Deer thought about this as he stumbled through the forest on his wobbly new legs.

"Then, if it's that way," he said out loud to himself, "I'll be named 'Clumsy' or 'Bumper' or 'Straddle-Bug.'"

"Why?" said Buffin, popping his head out from the hollow log.

"Just watch the way I jump, if you want to know," said Little Deer. "Watch!"

He wobbled up to the hollow log, gave a weak little jump, and landed right on top of it. Then he squirmed and wiggled over and fell on the other side, with his legs all ways.

"You can't jump because you think you can't," said Buffin, starting down the path to Rushing Brook.

"I think I can't because I *can't*," said Little Deer, picking himself up and following.

Down by the brook they found a bush covered with big ripe blackberries. It was very quiet in the

forest as they stood on the bank, munching the
juicy berries. Not a breeze was stirring the trees,
and the only sound was the rushing of the brook.

All of a sudden came the sharp snap of a twig.
Little Deer was so startled that he sailed into the
air like a bird and came down on the opposite bank.

Then he turned to see what had made the noise, and there stood his mother beside Buffin.

"How would you like to be called 'White-tailed Flier'?" she asked.

But Little Deer couldn't answer a word—because it was such a *beautiful* name.

SQUIFFY MAKES A RESCUE

SQUIFFY was a show-off. When he was a little baby, he began it. "Such a show-off," all the animals said.

"Watch me!" he said one day in the nest. His little sisters watched with wide eyes while he climbed up the side.

"Look!" he shouted. "Famous Flying Squirrel!" He jumped into the air and landed with a flop on his sisters. They said, "Ouch, my back!" and things like that. But Puff, the littlest one, said, "He *did* almost fly!"

That wasn't enough for Squiffy. The next day he said, "Stand back and look at the Great Twirler!" So they stood back and watched him jump up high and twirl around once before coming down. It was a handsome stunt, but he came down PLOP on the head of Mother Squirrel, who was just coming in the door.

"You looked nice up there, twirling," said Puff.

"Show-offs are bad," said Mother Squirrel, when her head was better. "Show-offs are silly. They say, 'Look at me' when there are silly things to do, but when there are *important* things to do, they just sit down and curl their tails around them."

That was a long speech for Mother Squirrel, and Squiffy thought about it in his bed that night.

The next day, although it was raining, Mother Squirrel went out to get pussy-willow buds for dinner. When she had been gone a long time, the

little squirrels suddenly noticed that Puff was no longer in the nest. They rushed to the door and looked down, and there, sitting in a cold puddle and weeping besides, was the littlest sister.

There was a great chatter in the nest. It was raining hard and the puddle was getting deeper and everything was dreadful.

Squiffy had never been to the ground before, but he put his back feet out over the edge and started backing down the tree. Halfway down he let go and dropped into the puddle with Puff.

Puff climbed onto his back and held on tight while Squiffy dug his nails in and climbed up the tree as far as the first branch. There he rested, and then he climbed to the second branch. He could hear his sisters crying and chattering above.

On the third try he reached the doorway and dumped Puff over the edge into the nest.

When Mother Squirrel came home and saw Puff all wet and shivering, she said, "Squiffy, what have you been up to?" But Squiffy just sat down and curled his tail around him.

Then his little sisters said, "He did a *very important thing!* And this time he didn't say 'Watch me!'—not once!"

water hole to show his blue jacket to the zebras, giraffes, and little hippos. As Bobo was strutting around, being admired by all the animals, something DREADFUL happened!

Bobo slipped on a log and fell
—*SPLASH!*—into the muddy
water.

When he got up, he looked at his lovely blue jacket. It was all covered with sticky brown mud.

The other animals laughed, but Bobo didn't. He cried!

He trotted home to his mother, crying all the way.

"Don't cry, Little Bobo," said his mother. "We'll take your blue jacket to the laundry and have it

washed until it is as good as new."

So Bobo's mother started off
with the muddy blue jacket in her
trunk, and Bobo trotted along beside her. Soon they came to the

old monkey's laundry under the big
baobab tree.

"Can you wash Little Bobo's

blue jacket, quick as a wink?" asked
Bobo's mother. And she showed
the jacket to the old monkey.

But the old monkey was a little hard of hearing and, besides, he was splashing so loudly in his washtub that he thought Bobo's mother said, "Can you wash Little Bobo's blue jacket and make it shrink?"

So the old monkey scrubbed the jacket in very soapy water, with a whole bottle of "Shrinko" in it.

And when the blue jacket was washed and ironed, it was so small that the smallest elephant in the world couldn't have worn it.

When Bobo saw his blue
jacket again, he cried!
His mother cried, too!

Even the old monkey cried into his washtub, until it overflowed!

At last Bobo stopped crying and said, "If *I* can't wear my lovely blue jacket, maybe I can give it to someone who *can!*"

So he asked the little giraffe
to try it on. But the blue jacket was
too small for him.

The little zebra tried it on, but
it was too small for *him*.

It was too small for the little lion.

It was too small for the little
tiger. And it was too small for the
little hippo!

Then a tear trickled down Bobo's cheek and he sobbed, "Isn't there *anyone*, *anywhere*, who *can* wear my lovely blue jacket with the two big pockets?"

"I hope *I* can," panted Big Brother Hippo, who had come running when he heard that Bobo wanted to give his jacket away. "I've *always* wanted a lovely blue jacket with two big pockets."

Big Brother Hippo picked up the blue jacket and pushed and wriggled and shoved until he got one front leg into a sleeve of the jacket.

Then he pushed and wriggled
and shoved some more, and pulled
and struggled until he got the other
front leg into the other sleeve of
the jacket.

But the jacket was so very tight
that Big Brother Hippo couldn't
move a muscle. He would have
been standing right there yet if
Bobo hadn't pulled it off.

Then Bobo looked at the blue
jacket. Somehow it looked bigger.
It WAS bigger! Big Brother Hippo

had tried so hard to get the jacket on that he had stretched it. So Bobo tried it on himself. And it JUST EXACTLY FITTED HIM!

And Bobo was so happy to be able to wear his blue jacket with the two big pockets again—that he even wore it to bed that night!

Mommy Cat and Her Kittens

W ASH YOUR dirty faces and paws," meowed Mommy Cat to her three kittens one night. "It is time for bed."

"I am too tired," said Timmie. "I'm so sleepy I can't even wash a whisker."

"Me too," mewed Tammie and Tommie.

"I don't see why you kittens are so tired," said Mommy Cat. "Tomorrow I am going to find out. I will do everything that you do. We will play together all day long. Then perhaps I will see what makes you so tired at night."

"You will have lots of fun!" said Tammie.

The kittens curled up in the basket. Mommy Cat poked out her pink tongue and washed the kittens, one by one. She licked Tammie until she was white and fluffy. She scrubbed Tommie until his black fur was clean and shiny. Mommy Cat rested her tired tongue, then washed yellow

Timmie, who was dirtiest of all. Then Mommy Cat curled up around her kittens and they all went to sleep.

The kittens awakened early next morning. After breakfast, they scampered to the barn. Mommy Cat followed them.

"Up into the hayloft!" said Timmie, so up into the hayloft they all went. They tumbled about in the hay, playing hide and seek. When Mommy Cat tried to hide, the hay tickled her nose and made her sneeze. It was easy to find Mommy Cat.

The kittens just listened for sneezes, and found her right away!

"Now let's play tag," said Timmie. "You're 'it,' Mommy Cat!"

Away went the kittens, out of the hayloft. Away went Mommy Cat, after the kittens.

Mommy Cat ran and ran. She chased Tommie in and out of the meadow, but she couldn't catch him. She chased Timmie around and around the barn, but she couldn't catch him. Mommy Cat was getting tired. She went into the woods and sat

down behind a tree to rest. Just then, Tammie crept quietly past the tree.

"You're 'it'!" yowled Mommy Cat, and she pounced out and tagged Tammie on the tail.

"Let's all rest for awhile," said Mommy Cat. "Time for a cat nap!"

"All right," said the kittens, and they curled up and went to sleep. Mommy Cat sighed as she closed her tired eyes. In less than five minutes, the three kittens were wide awake.

"Nap time is over!" said Tommie. "Time to play again!"

"That wasn't a cat nap at all," said Mommy Cat sleepily. "That was just a wee kitten nap!"

All afternoon, Mommy Cat and the kittens played together.

They climbed trees in the orchard.

They chased a yellow
butterfly and a squirmy
black bug.

They ran after pigs
and made them grunt
"Oink."

They chased lambs
and made them say
"Baa-baa."

They chased chickens
and made them say
"Cluck-cluck-cluck!"

The kittens turned somersaults and flip-flops and rolled in the grass. They batted at one another with their soft, furry paws.

Everything the kittens did, Mommy Cat did, too. She bounced and pounced and leaped and

tumbled. She turned somersaults and flip-flops and rolled in the grass. She batted at the kittens with her soft, furry paws.

Mommy Cat moved more and more slowly. At last she lay down and sighed a tired sigh.

"Let's race to the house and see if supper is ready," said Tammie.

Away ran the kittens. Mommy Cat followed slowly behind. She was so tired that her tummy touched the ground as she dragged herself along. As soon as supper was over, she crawled into the basket.

"Time to wash your paws and faces," said Mommy Cat with a yawn.

"We aren't sleepy," said Tommie. "We want to play some more."

"No!" said Mommy Cat. "Wash yourselves and get right to sleep!" Mommy Cat looked so cross that the kittens started washing as fast as they could!

Mommy Cat sat with her eyes half closed, rocking back and forth.

"You had better wash, too," said Tammie. "You are as dirty as can be!"

"I'm too tired," said Mommy Cat, and she closed her eyes and slid down into the bottom of the basket.

"Mommy Cat always washes *us* when *we* are tired," said Timmie.

"We can't have Mommy Cat going to bed *dirty*," said Tommie.

"There is just one thing to do," said Tammie.

The three little kittens poked out their pink
tongues and started to work.

They washed Mommy Cat's dear, dirty face.
They scrubbed her tired, dirty paws. They crawled
around on top of Mommy Cat, washing as they

went. Their tongues got so tired they could hardly move them, but they kept on scrubbing.

They washed and wiped and licked and scrubbed until Mommy Cat was clean and fluffy and yellow as butter . . . and sound asleep all over.

And so were the three little kittens.

This Book Belongs To:

_____